# NOBODY KNOWS
# I HAVE DELICATE TOES

# NOBODY KNOWS
# I HAVE DELICATE TOES

# by Nancy Patz

**Franklin Watts**
New York | London
Toronto | Sydney | 1980

Library of Congress Cataloging in Publication Data

Patz, Nancy.
   Nobody knows I have delicate toes.

   SUMMARY: Benjamin and his friend, an elephant,
get in and out of trouble while getting ready for bed.
   [1. Night—Fiction. 2. Elephants—Fiction]
I. Title.
PZ7.P27833No        [E]            79-16304
ISBN 0-531-02392-3
ISBN 0-531-04096-8 lib. bdg.

**Also by Nancy Patz**
*Pumpernickel Tickle and Mean Green Cheese*

To Susan and Jeanne

One night just before bedtime
Benjamin and Elephant were busy as usual.

"Get ready for bed now, Benjamin!" Benjamin's mother called.
"Clean up your room and take your bath."

"It's early, Mom!" called Benjamin.

"NOW!" said Benjamin's mother.

"I'd better get ready
for bed, El."

"I'll help you, Benj,"
said Elephant.

"Where does the ball
belong, Benj?"

"Back in the box
in the corner, El."

"I'll bounce the ball
and hop a hop
and *plop!* the ball
goes into the box."

"Good shot, El!"
said Benjamin.

"Where does the orange truck go, Benj?"

"Right up there on the middle shelf."

"I'll help you, Benj," said Elephant.
"I'll jiggle and juggle a bit with my trunk
  and tap it and tip it
  till *plinkitty-plunk*,
  it settles itself away on the shelf."

"I'm a good helper,
  aren't I, Benj?"

"You bet, El,"
said Benjamin.

And everything went fine until...

Elephant yelled, "FOUR! THREE! TWO! ONE! BLAST-OFF!"
He zoomed a rocket across the room and...

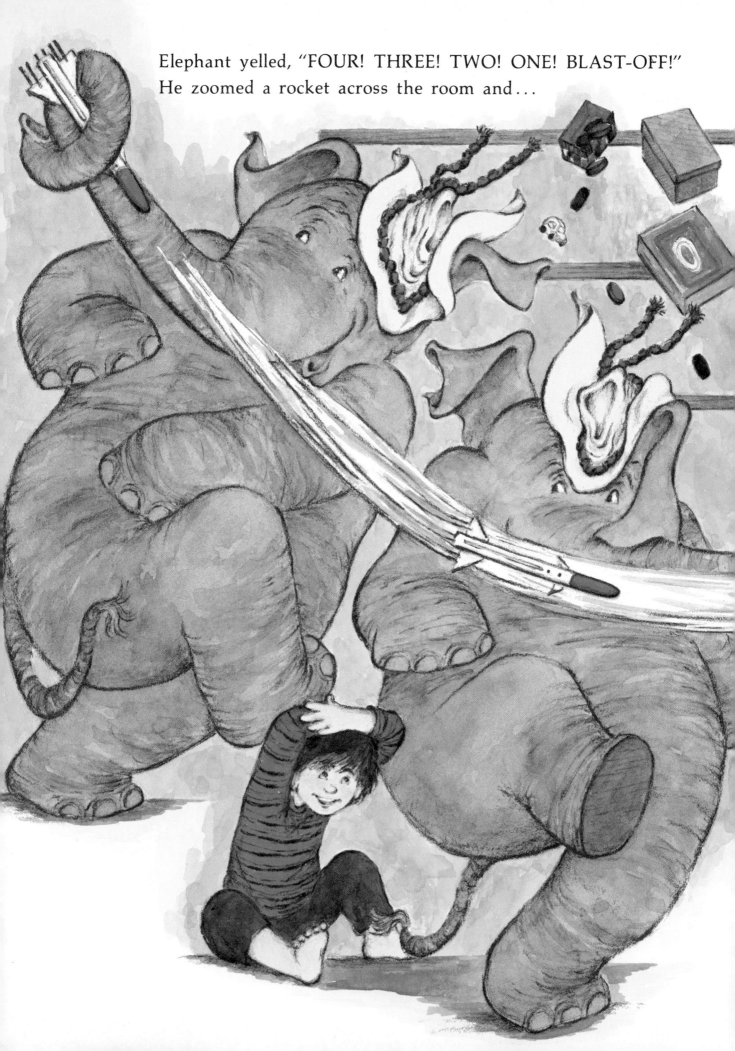

bumped — THUNK! — into the shelves.
And everything came tumbling down.

Elephant stumbled
   and tripped on his trunk
      and crashed with a thundering roar!

"WHAT'S GOING ON IN THERE,
BENJAMIN?"

"Elephant, you're not helping at all!" fussed
Benjamin. "You're going to get me in trouble."

And Benjamin put the toys away.

"I couldn't have
done it better myself,"
said Elephant.

"HAVE YOU TAKEN
YOUR BATH YET,
BENJAMIN?"

"I think I'd better
take my bath."

"I'll help you, Benj,"
said Elephant.

"I hope this soap is good for my trunk.
I do have a delicate elephant trunk."

"I didn't know that," said Benjamin.

"*Nobody* knows," said Elephant. "And nobody knows
I have delicate toes."

"Nobody knows you have delicate toes?"

"That's right, Benj," said Elephant.

"And nobody sees I have delicate knees!"

"You're kidding me, El!"

"Would I do that?" laughed Elephant.

"Delicate elephant!"

"Elegant nose!"

"Delicate elephant
knees and toes!"

Such a good time
in the tub!
Until...

"ARE
 YOU
 READY
 FOR
 BED
 YET,
 BENJAMIN?
 I'LL
 BE
 THERE
 IN
 A
 MINUTE!"

Elephant hid under the water like a submarine.

"I'm practically ready!"
Benjamin hollered.

Then he yelled, "Get moving, El!"

But Elephant was stuck in the tub!

Absolutely stuck in the tub.

Benjamin pushed.

Benjamin tugged.

But he couldn't get Elephant unplugged.

"What are we going to do, Benj?"

"We'll have to think of something, El."

Elephant moaned.

But Benjamin was thinking.

And he got a good idea.

He said, "Pull yourself up
by the bar up there."

"The bar up where?"

"The bar up there."

"I'll try, Benj," said Elephant.

Benjamin gave him a push from the side.

But Elephant stayed stuck.

# "BENJAMIN, ARE YOU READY?"

"We've got to think of something, El!"

"I did, but I just forgot it, Benj."

"Elephants never forget, El."

"They do when they're upset, Benj,"
said Elephant.

Elephant was upset.

But Benjamin was thinking.

And he got a good idea.

"I hope this soap
   is a slippery soap," said Benjamin.

"I hope so, too," said Elephant.

And together they soaped Elephant all over.

"Let's try it again, El!" Benjamin yelled.

So they pushed and they pulled...

and nothing happened at all.

So they pushed and pulled
some more.

And nothing happened at all.
Until...

SPLUSH!

"I knew we could do it,
El!" laughed Benjamin.

"Me, too, Benj,"
said Elephant.

Elephant slurped the puddles up
and squirted all the water
back into the tub.

They mopped the floor
and got themselves
ready for...

bed.

"Did you take a good bath,
Benjamin?" asked Benjamin's mother.

"You bet, Mom!" said Benjamin.

And Benjamin and Elephant
smiled.